DOUBLES TROUBLE

BY JAKE MADDOX

Text by Blake Hoena
Illustrated by Sean Tiffany

STONE ARCH BOOKS
a capstone imprint

Jake Maddox Sports Stories are published by
Stone Arch Books
a Capstone Imprint
1710 Roe Crest Drive
North Mankato, Minnesota 56003

www.mycapstone.com

Library of Congress Cataloguing-in-Publication Data is available on the Library of Congress website.

ISBN: 978-1-4965-4957-0 (library binding)
ISBN: 978-1-4965-4959-4 (paperback)
ISBN: 978-1-4965-4961-7 (eBook PDF)

Summary: Deion tries out for the traveling team playing singles but doesn't make the cut. When his coach points him toward the possibility of playing doubles, Deion finds a new but troublesome option.

Editor: Nate LeBoutillier
Designer: Lori Bye
Production Specialist: Tori Abraham

Printed in Canada.
010382F17

TABLE OF CONTENTS

CHAPTER 1

TENNIS CLUB CHAMP

Deion watched Trey step up to the baseline. Deion noticed the nervous glance that his opponent cast his way.

I own him, Deion thought confidently.

"Thirty–forty," said Mr. Sumner, their phys ed teacher. Then he added, "Match point."

Deion shifted his weight from foot to foot. He was loose. He was ready. He was on the verge of breaking his opponent's serve and winning the match.

Whack!

The ball sped toward Deion, but he easily handled the serve.

Whack!

Deion returned the ball.

Trey scrambled to the far corner get to it and sent a weak shot back to Deion.

I got him now, Deion thought.

Whack!

Deion knocked the ball deep to the baseline. Then he charged the net. Trey wheeled backward. He was off balance when he hit the ball. A high-arching lob sailed right to Deion.

Smack!

Deion spiked the ball with an overhand slam. The ball rocketed past Trey, hitting the back fence with a satisfying *ching!*

Deion ran to the net to shake Trey's hand. "Great match," he said.

"Thanks. You, too," Trey replied.

Mr. Sumner called the members of their school's tennis club to gather round. There were eight kids in all.

Trey and Deion's school had only two courts, and they were in rough shape. The nets sagged, and the lines needed to be repainted. But a group of kids had been interested in learning to play, so the school let them start a tennis club. Mr. Sumner served as the club's advisor.

"This was a great first year for the tennis club," Mr. Sumner said. "And what an exciting way to end the school year, with a tournament." He pulled out a small plastic trophy. "This year's champ, Deion Carr," he announced.

The other kids clapped as Deion accepted his prize.

Afterward, everyone went to gather up their gear, but Deion hung back.

"What's up?" Mr. Sumner asked, walking over to Deion.

Deion sighed.

With school ending, Deion doubted he would have anyone to play tennis with. His friends just played hoops all summer.

"I wish the club didn't have to end just because school's out," he said.

"If you want to keep working on your game, head down to the rec center next Friday," Mr. Sumner said. "I coach a local rec team, and you could tryout."

"Really?" Deion said. "That'd be great!"

"But if you try out, you have to call me Coach," Mr. Sumner said, smiling. "I'm only Mr. Sumner during the school year."

"Thanks, Mr. Sumner," Deion replied. "I mean . . . Coach."

CHAPTER 2

REC TEAM TRYOUT

The next Friday, Deion biked down to the rec center. That's how he ended up on the opposite side of the net from Ryan, a kid with a cannon of a serve.

Whack!

Ryan's serve rocketed toward Deion, curving across the centerline. Deion had just a fraction second to react, to get his racket around.

Thwack!

Deion smacked the ball over the net, but his shot went wide.

"Out!" called Ryan.

Deion scratched his head. Ryan's serve seemed impossible to return. Mr. Sumner sat nearby and watched Deion's match closely.

Ryan strutted back up to the service line. "Forty–love," he said. He casually bounced the ball on the court, and then he looked over at Deion. Just before he served, he smiled.

Whack!

The serve was a yellow streak whizzing over the net. Luckily for Deion, it landed just beyond the service line.

"Out!" called Deion.

Okay, now's my chance, Deion thought. *Time to impress.*

Ryan's second serve came in slower. Deion easily got his racket on it and returned the ball deep. Then he charged the net, hoping to catch his opponent off guard. But Ryan blasted the ball down the sideline, past Deion's reach. Deion could only turn and watch as the ball landed in behind him.

Deion groaned.

As the boys changed sides, Deion saw Mr. Sumner scribbling something in a notepad. He hated to think what Mr. Sumner might be writing about him.

Deion fared slighly better when it was his turn to serve. He scored a couple points but still lost the game. As he prepared to receive Ryan's serve again, he noticed that Mr. Sumner had moved on to watch some kids playing on another court.

Deion felt discouraged. His tryout was not going as he had hoped. At school, he had dominated his classmates. He had thought he stood a good chance to make the rec center team. But the kids going out for the squad were stiffer completion than he had faced in his school's tennis club.

"Okay, Deion, I've seen enough for today," Mr. Sumner said before it was Deion's turn to serve again. "Glad you could come try out."

Then Mr. Sumner went to talk to Ryan.

Deion felt embarrassed about how his tryout went. He left without even saying good-bye to Mr. Sumner.

CHAPTER 3

THE CALL

That night at dinner, Deion's phone buzzed. He expected his mom to be annoyed that he forgot to turn it off. His stepdad, Terry, looked up from his spaghetti, and he said, "If it's about your tryout, you can answer it."

Deion looked to his mom to make sure it was okay. She nodded. Then Deion dug his phone out of his pocket. The caller ID showed Mr. Sumner's name.

"Hey, Coach," Deion said, answering the phone.

"Deion, sorry, I never got a chance to talk to you after tryouts," Mr. Sumner said.

"That's okay," Deion replied.

Then there was a long pause.

Deion knew what was coming next. It would be bad news.

"Well, I just wanted to tell you that all the singles spots on the team are filled," Mr. Sumner said.

Deion looked down at his food. He didn't want to see anyone watching him.

"But if you're interested," Mr. Sumner went on to say, "I could use a team assistant. Someone to help with equipment and keep score. You could even get some practice in with the team."

"Thanks, Coach," Deion said. "I'll think about it."

Mr. Sumner and Deion said goodbye.

"Well?" Deion's mom asked.

Deion shook his head.

"I can dust off my racket if you want to play sometime," Terry said.

Deion was not sure what to think of that offer. His mom had remarried a few months ago, and Deion had known the guy for about a year before that. But Terry still felt like a stranger to Deion. They just had not found anything to bond over. While Terry was a football fanatic, Deion didn't care much for the sport. Terry was a bookworm, but Deion was more into music.

Deion figured the offer to play tennis was just an attempt to find something in common with him.

"Sure, let's play someday," Deion said quietly, and then he went back to eating.

CHAPTER 4

THE TEXT

Deion never told his mom or Terry about Mr. Sumner's offer. He did not think being an assistant was something that he wanted to do, especially since he did not know any of the other guys on the squad. He would rather spend the summer hanging out with his friends and playing basketball.

But by Thursday, Deion still had not told Mr. Sumner about his decision. He was putting it off, afraid Mr. Sumner would be disappointed.

Then he received a surprise text.

Hey, it's Cole. Coach gave me your number.

Deion did not remember a Cole from tryouts, but he replied, *What's up?*

Wanna be my doubles partner? Cole asked.

But I didn't make the team, Deion replied

Just meet me at the rec center, 11 tomorrow, Cole texted back.

Okay, Deion replied.

Deion stared at his phone, confused. He had never played doubles before, so why would Mr. Sumner have Cole contact him?

Just then, Terry walked by. He was holding an old, wooden tennis racket that was literally covered in dust.

"Up for some tennis?" Terry asked. "Found my racket out in the garage. Along with some other things that I still need to unpack."

Deion shook his head. "Nah, I'm good."

"Oh," Terry said. "Okay. We'll try another time, maybe."

Deion watched as Terry turned, with slumped shoulders, and walked away.

Deion knew that Terry was probably just trying to connect, to be helpful.

But from the look of that old wooden racket, Terry probably hadn't played in years. Deion couldn't imagine that playing tennis with Terry would go well.

CHAPTER 5

MEET AND GREET

The next day, Deion biked down to the rec center. He rolled up to the tennis courts and then leaned his bike against the fence.

There were seven guys on the courts. Deion did not know what Cole looked like, but on one court, one guy was playing against two.

Cole must be the odd man out, Deion thought. He walked over to that court and said, "Hey, I'm Deion."

"Cool you could make it," a short, blond-haired kid said. "I'm Cole. Soon as you're ready, you can hop in with me."

A few minutes later, Deion had changed shoes and stretched out. He was ready to go.

"Front or back?" Cole asked.

"Huh?" Deion said. He was not sure what Cole was asking.

"You take the net," Cole said. Cole pointed up front as he backed up behind the baseline.

"I've never played doubles before," Deion said.

Cole shrugged. "Then you'll learn."

One of the guys on the other side of the net served to Cole. Cole easily returned the ball.

When the opponents hit the ball back, it went wide of Deion. He watched it land outside the singles sideline but in the doubles alley.

Their opponents high-fived.

"Aw, man!" Deion said. Then turning to Cole, he said, "Sorry, I'm used to letting those go."

"No worries," Cole said. "It's just for fun."

Deion wished he could have more fun. It seemed like everything he did was a mistake.

While playing the net, he reached up for a shot that was lobbed over his head and hit the ball out of bounds.

"Don't forget that I'm back here, Deion," Cole said, laughing.

"Yeah, sorry," Deion replied.

The very next point, Deion foolishly reached across the centerline and knocked a shot wide. After doing so, he immediately realized that Cole could have easily gotten to the ball.

Thankfully, Cole was good-natured about it. "Just remember there's two of us," Cole joked. "You don't need to cover the whole court like in singles."

After playing a set and losing 6-1, Cole introduced Deion to their opponents.

"Meet Brandon and Travis," Cole said, pointing to their opponents. "They're on the twelve-and-under squad."

Deion said hello. But knowing their age made Deion feel even worse. He was getting shown up by kids younger than him.

Then he met the guys playing on the other court. Two of them were on the 14U squad and two were on the 12U.

After the introductions were over, they switched opponents. Cole and Deion played a set against the two other 14U players.

Deion thought he played better. At least he didn't get in Cole's way as much. But they still lost the set, 6-2.

Afterward, the eight boys gathered around to chat.

"So what do you think?" Cole asked. "Is Deion on the team?"

The other guys answered with nods and positive murmurs.

"So you in?" Cole asked Deion.

"Don't I need to tryout or something?" Deion asked.

"You just did," Cole said.

As Cole and Deion chatted, the other boys wondered off. Deion was confused. He had played horribly, he thought. But this kid still wanted to be his partner.

"If you don't want to play doubles, I get it," Cole said with a smirk. "It's not as high-profile as singles. I mean, nobody knows who the Wimbledon doubles champions are."

"No, no. That's not it," Deion said. "You lost to a couple twelve-year-olds because of me."

"You mean Travis and Brandon?" Cole asked. "Do you know how many tournaments they've won? I wish I could be as good at doubles as they are."

"Okay, still," Deion said. "I bombed."

"Coach said your game needs polishing," Cole said. "But he also said you had potential."

"Really?" Deion said. A mix of pride and embarrassment caused him to blush. He didn't realize that Mr. Sumner talked about him. Or that he saw promise in his game.

"So you need some net time, and I need a doubles partner," Cole said.

"Okay, I'm in," Deion said.

Deion didn't know why, but he found himself extendeding a handshake toward Cole.

Cole shook Deion's hand.

The small gesture seemed to make it official. Deion was on the team, and he was going to be Cole's doubles partner.

CHAPTER 6

DOUBLES SURPRISE

Next Monday, practice officially began. Deion was excited to be on the team. He got to the rec center early. To his surprise, most of the team was already there, stretching out and chatting.

Deion walked over to Cole. On the way, he spotted Mr. Sumner.

"Hey, Coach," he said.

"Good to see you, Deion," Mr. Sumner said. "I was really hoping that you would partner up with Cole."

"But we never played doubles at school," Deion said.

"Cole will show you the ropes," Mr. Sumner said. "He's one of my best players."

"Really?" Deion asked.

Mr. Sumner answered with a nod.

Deion felt both thankful and a little scared at having Cole as his partner. It was great to be paired up with a skilled player. But he also felt pressure to play up to Cole's level.

Practice started with warm-ups.

First, Mr. Sumner had them work the legs with lunges and footwork drills. Then they worked their arms and shoulders. It was similar to what Mr. Sumner had them do in tennis club but much more intense.

After warm-ups, Mr. Sumner had them practice volleying. They took turns, with one player lobbing the ball to a teammate. The other player would then return it over the net. At one point, Mr. Sumner stopped to watch Deion as he tapped a lobbed ball back over the net.

"Deion, don't just hit the ball over the net," he said. "Plant your feet and then knock it over like you're in the middle of the match."

"Okay, Coach," Deion said.

"Remember, train with a purpose," Mr. Sumner yelled out. "How you practice will reflect how you play."

That was a big part of Mr. Sumner's message. He did not want his players to hit the ball around half-heartedly. He wanted them to practice as intensely as they would play during a match.

The team's practice was nothing like tennis club. At school, Mr. Sumner was mostly concerned with teaching kids the basics of the game and having fun. Here, he was teaching them how to play like pros.

Deion was sweating and exhausted by the end.

"Okay," Mr Sumner said, "gather round, team. Our first matches will be in a week, so we'll need to get some practice in. We'll rotate between singles and doubles, with singles Tuesdays and Thursdays. Doubles on Wednesdays and Fridays. But you are always welcome to hang out and help at any practice."

As Deion was getting on his bike, Cole walked up to him. "So what did you think of practice?" he asked.

"That was intense," Deion replied.

"Yeah, Coach knows how to motivate us to play well," Cole said. "I've really upped my game thanks to him."

As they were talking, Ryan, the kid with the cannon for a serve, walked by. He nodded at Cole but did not acknowledge Deion.

"I played against him at tryouts," Deion said. "He's really good. But what's his deal?"

"Ryan?" Cole said. "He made the starting squad last year, so thinks he runs the team."

"He does have a killer serve," Deion said.

"The game of tennis involves more than just serving," Cole said.

CHAPTER 7

PRACTICE LIKE YOU PLAY

Deion decided to check out singles practice. He thought he might be able to help Mr. Sumner and also pick up a few pointers. When he got there, he was surprised to see Cole stretching out.

"Are you here to help with practice too?" Deion asked.

Cole shook his head. "Nah, I play singles."

"Coach has you doing both?" Deion said.

"I played singles last year," Cole said. "But Coach thought playing doubles would help me focus more on my shot placement. Plus, it gives me more court time."

Mr. Sumner walked up to them. "Nice to see you, Deion," he said. "You here to help out?"

Deion nodded, and Mr. Sumner quickly put him to work. He hit serves to other players, so they could work on their returns. He gathered loose balls while the singles players worked on volleying at the net.

The day ended with some practices sets. Deion took a seat in the judge's chair to keep score for the players. At one point, Cole and Ryan faced off.

Ryan served first.

Whack!

The serve scorched over the net. Deion was impressed by Ryan's power. Amazingly, Cole got his racket in front of the ball for a solid return shot.

Whack!

Cole sent the ball to Ryan's backhand. Ryan looked a little surprised that Cole had returned his serve so easily.

Thwack!

Ryan sent his shot wide. Deion watched the ball bounce toward the fence.

"Hey, call out the score," Ryan shouted to Deion. He sounded annoyed.

"Sorry," Deion called out. "Love–fifteen,"

Whack!

Ryan's serve went long.

"Fault!" Deion shouted.

Ryan's second serve was softer because he did not want to double fault and give Cole the point.

Cole wound up on the ball with a strong, two-handed forehand return.

Whack!

Cole's return sizzled down the sideline just out of Ryan's reach.

"Hey, we're just practicing!" Ryan yelled.

"Coach always says to practice like you play," Cole said. Then he looked over at Deion and smiled.

"Love–thirty," Deion called out.

Cole's comment seemed to motivate Ryan. He rocketed his next serve past Cole for an easy ace.

"Fifteen–thirty," Deion called out.

The ball whizzed back and forth over the net as the two volleyed. And the set turned out to be a close one. Cole had a 5-3 lead when Mr. Sumner called everyone in to end the practice.

Luckily for Ryan, it probably saved him some embarrassment.

CHAPTER 8

ARE YOU GAME?

After a few doubles practices, Deion felt more confident in his game. He was learning when to get the ball and when to trust his partner to get it. Doubles demanded a surprising level of communication and teamwork, which made playing a lot of fun. By the day of his first official match, Deion felt like he was ready to take on anyone.

That morning at breakfast, Terry sat down at the table across from Deion.

"Like a ride to the rec center?" he asked.

"Nah, I'll bike down," Deion replied.

"Okay," Terry said. "Then your mom and I will drive down later to see you play."

Deion just nodded.

Deion hopped on his bike and headed for the rec center. He wanted to get there early, so he could watch the singles matches and cheer on his teammates.

As he pedaled along, Deion thought about different tennis strategies, situations, and shots. He was lost in thought for a good ten minutes before he even realized it. All this tennis action had become more than just a hobby.

When Deion arrived at the rec center, he saw Cole. He was alone and stretching out.

Deion looked around. "Your parents here?"

"Nah," Cole replied. "My dad's stationed overseas, so I don't see him much. And my mom, she works a lot."

Cole frowned after his comment. Deion could tell that he might have brought up a sore subject. He knew a thing or two about unsettled parental situations.

"Well," said Deion, trying to lighten the mood, "I guess it's a good thing I'm here to cheer you on."

Cole smiled at that. Then Deion ran off to see if Mr. Sumner needed any help.

The matches started off in successful fashion for their team. Cole easily won his, 6-2, 6-3. Ryan also won his match, but in three sets. One of the other 14U singles players won, and the other lost. The results were the same for the 12U kids: three wins and one loss. Their squad was doing well.

No matter how things were going, Mr. Sumner was always coaxing his players on. He was supportive and inspired everyone to play their very best.

After the singles matches, there was a break so the doubles players could warm up. That's when Deion saw his mom and Terry walking over to the courts. They waved, and he nodded.

Before their first match, Deion asked Cole, "Are you game for this?"

"Always," Cole said, bumping Deion's fist.

The other team served first, Cole was set to receive.

Whack!

Cole returned it back to the server.

Whack!

The server blasted the ball down the sideline, to Deion's backhand. He was caught off guard at how quickly the ball came back to him and could not get his racket on it. He turned to see Cole scrambling for the ball. It landed in and bounced past his teammate.

"Fifteen–love!"

It was Deion's turn to receive the serve. He stepped back behind the baseline. He shifted his weight from foot to foot. He felt loose. He felt ready.

Whack!

The ball was a yellow streak. But this kid did not have the killer serve that Ryan had. Deion got his racket around on the ball.

Whack!

He hit it directly at the opponent who was playing the net.

Smack!

The kid hit a perfect cross-court shot, which went right between Cole and Deion.

"Thirty–love"

The rest of the game went pretty much the same way. Deion missed a couple shots, and they lost. The score was 0-1.

Cole served next, and he was on. Deion barely had to touch the ball. And just like that, the score was tied 1-1.

Their opponents held serve. It was 1-2.

CHAPTER 9

AUSTRALIAN RULES DOUBLES

Overall, the team did well. Deion was happy about that, but he could not help feeling disappointed at his poor showing. As his teammates headed out, Deion hung back. Cole stayed with him.

"So what do you think?" Cole asked.

"That was rough," Deion said. "I kind of feel like I failed you."

"Hey, it's just the first match of the summer," Cole said. "There's always next week."

"Yeah, I suppose," Deion said. But he was worried that he'd let Cole down again.

Terry walked up. "What are you boys doing tomorrow?" he asked.

"I don't know," Cole said. "Nothing."

Deion shrugged.

"Then let's meet here tomorrow around one o'clock, okay?" Terry said. "Bring your gear."

"Sure," Cole replied.

The next day, Terry drove Deion down to the rec center. He didn't know what Terry had planned until he saw him pull a duffel bag out of the trunk. The handle of his ancient wooden tennis racket stuck out of it.

As they walked over to the courts, Deion heard the screech of a city bus stopping in front of the rec center. Out hopped Cole with his gear bag. He ran over to join them.

"Hey, Cole," Terry said. "I'm going to introduce you two to Australian rules doubles."

Terry explained that Australian rules doubles was a way for three people to play by rotating who served. To start off, Terry served to Cole and Deion.

Whack!

The ball sped toward Cole. He returned it deep to Terry's backhand.

Whack!

Terry hit the ball over down the center

Whack!

Deion was at the net and saw his chance. He tapped the ball with his racket.

Tink!

The ball dropped softly on the other side of the net and bounced a couple times before Terry could get to it.

"Nice one," Terry said.

Then he served to Deion.

Whack!

Deion got his racket around on the ball. He returned it right to Terry, who knocked the ball down the sideline past Cole.

"Great shot!" Cole said.

As they played on, Deion could tell that his stepdad was a bit rusty. Terry missed a few easy shots and wasn't putting a lot of power on the ball. But his aim was deadly. He snuck a couple shots down the sideline that took Cole and Deion by surprise.

Still, they were able to break his serve.

"Okay, so now it's Deion's turn to serve to me and Cole," Terry said as he joined Cole on one side of the court.

Deion changed sides and served to Cole.

Whack!

Cole returned a soft shot to Deion.

As he waited for the ball to bounce in front of him, Deion surveyed the court in front of him. Terry was at the net on the right. Cole was on the left, trying to recover.

Whack!

Deion hit a crosscourt forehand that landed in the back corner of the doubles alley. Cole had no time to get to it, and the ball bounced to the fence.

"Fifteen–love!" Deion called out happily.

"Look who's getting cocky," Terry said.

When Deion served to his stepdad, Terry returned it down the sideline, out of reach.

Cole and Terry eventually broke Deion's serve, too. Then it was Cole's serve. Terry lost the handle on his racket and sent one of Cole's serves sailing over the fence. Cole ran after it.

"You know," Terry said to Deion, "Cole's really thankful to have you as a partner."

"I doubt that," Deion said. "We lost our first match because of me."

"You have to remember, you're a team," Terry said. "And he couldn't play without you."

Deion shrugged dismissively.

"See, you play to win. That's what drives you," Terry continued. "But Cole, he plays for other reasons, for something to do."

That made Deion recall what Cole had said the other day. His dad wasn't around, and his mom worked a lot. Without the tennis team, Cole might be stuck at home by himself most of the summer.

When Cole returned to the court having fetched Terry's errant shot, he was giggling. "This isn't baseball, Terry," he said.

"Thought hitting it over the fence was a home run!" said Terry.

Even Deion chuckled at that one.

As Cole served out the rest of that game, Deion pondered. He began to open up to the idea that maybe Cole *was* happy to have him on his doubles team. Sure, without Deion, Cole could still be playing singles . . . and winning. But maybe what Cole needed was a partner.

The three of them kept at it until they were covered in sweat. When they were exhausted, they swapped out of their court shoes and chugged some water.

"That was a blast," Cole said. "Can we play Australian doubles again sometime?"

Terry turned to Deion and said, "What do you think? Want to do this again?"

Deion knew Terry wasn't just asking for Cole. He was also asking if Deion wanted to play with him again.

"Yeah, that'd be fun," Deion replied.

CHAPTER 10

TOURNAMENT TIME

Deion went through another week of practice. Then he and Cole played another match. They lost again, 6-3, 6-4, but at least they won a few more games.

The next week, Mr. Sumner announced that there would be a tournament over at East Dale Rec Center. "It's an open invite," he said, "so anyone who is interested in playing just needs to let me know."

Cole glanced over at Deion. "We in?"

Deion nodded.

They continued to practice. Then there was another weekend match. Deion and Cole lost again, but in three sets. They even pushed the last set to a tiebreaker.

While they had not won a match yet, Deion was feeling more confident. They were playing better. They were also having a lot of fun playing as partners.

They even managed to play some more Australian rules doubles with Terry. Deion was playing more tennis than he'd ever dreamed of. In fact, he was dreaming about it, too.

On the day of the tournament at the East Dale Rec Center, Terry offered to pick up Cole and drive the boys.

"Thanks, Terry," Cole said as he hopped into the back seat beside Deion.

"You game for this?" Deion asked, bumping Cole's fist.

"Always," Cole replied.

The East Dale Rec Center was a bigger venue than their local rec center. Instead of a couple metal bleachers, East Dale had actual stands.

61

That meant Deion and Cole would have a larger crowd watching their matches.

Their first opponents were a pair of mismatched kids. One was shorter than either Cole or Deion, and the other was much taller. The tall guy served first.

Whack!

The serve came in hot, but Cole was ready.

Whack!

Cole's return went deep, pushing the server beyond the baseline.

Whack!

The tall guy's return was hit down the center of the court, within Deion's reach.

Tink!

Deion angled his shot away from the player at the net, and it dropped in for a point. Cole and Deion exchanged a fist bump.

They kept the pressure on and broke their opponent's serve. Then they won Cole's serve but lost a game the next time their opponents served. Still, they had a 2-1 lead, and it was now Deion's serve.

This time, when he looked around to see all the strangers watching him, Deion focused on Terry sitting along the fence. That kept him from feeling so nervous.

Whack!

Deion's serve curved in.

Whack!

The short guy's return came back to Deion.

Whack!

Deion knocked it back to the short guy in the backcourt, but as he did, he saw the tall guy at the net creeping over.

I got him, Deion thought.

Whack!

The ball came right back to Deion. But this time, he drove it down the sideline, catching the taller player off guard. The ball sailed deep and landed just in-bounds.

"Nice shot, Deion!" said Cole.

"Thanks," said Deion. He took a ball out of his pocket and bounced it a few times before calling out, "Fifteen–love!"

They went on to win Deion's serve and eventually won the first set, 6-2.

Between sets, Mr. Sumner came up to them. "You guys are playing like you practice," he said, slapping them on the backs. "You're playing with intensity."

Cole walked over to the baseline to begin the second set. Before he served, he looked over at Deion, and asked, "Are you game for this?"

"I think we can win this thing," Deion said.

"You mean the entire tournament?" said Cole.

"Yep," said Deion. "The whole thing."

Cole smiled.

Deion walked up to the baseline. He felt loose. He felt ready.

I own them, he thought, looking over at his opponents.

Whack!

ALTERNATE TENNIS PLAY

Australian Doubles — three players compete, rotating servers. The server uses the singles lines on one side while the other two players use doubles alleys on the opposite side.

Mixed Doubles — teams have one male and one female player.

All-Court Tennis — one or more players compete against each other on either side of the net. The ball isn't dead until it rolls or is hit into the net. Shots may land anywhere on the court as long as they go over the net.

COMMON TENNIS TERMS

advantage—when a player needs one more point to win the game after the score was tied at deuce

alley—the extra area of the side court used for doubles

backhand—a tennis stroke made with the palm of the hand turned toward the body and the back of the hand facing the ball

baseline—the line indicating the back of the court

break—when the server loses the game

crosscourt—hitting the ball diagonally into the opponent's court

deuce—when the score in a game is tied at three or more points

double fault—two missed serves in a row resulting in the server losing a point

fault—a serve that is not in play

forehand—a tennis stroke made with the palm of the hand facing the ball

forty—number for three points scored in a game

lob—type of shot where the ball is lifted high above the net

love—zero points in a tennis game

thirty—number for two points scored in a game

volley—a shot where the ball hits a player's racket before it hits the ground

AUTHOR BIO

Sports were always a part of Blake Hoena's life whether he was bombing down a hill on his yellow penny board or cheering on his favorite football team. Today, he lives in St. Paul, Minnesota. He still rides a skateboard to get around and plays various sports from tennis to volleyball. When he's not playing or walking his dog, he's writing. Blake has written more than one hundred books for young readers.

ILLUSTRATOR BIO

Sean Tiffany has worked in the illustration and comic book field for more than twenty years. He has illustrated more than sixty children's books for Capstone and has been an instructor at the famed Joe Kubert School in northern New Jersey. Raised on a small island off the coast of Maine, Sean now resides in Boulder, Colorado, with his wife, Monika, their son, James, a cactus named Jim, and a room full of entirely too many guitars.

GLOSSARY

acknowledge—to admit the truth or existence of

fanatic—overly enthusiastic or devoted

intensity—extreme strength or force of feeling

murmur—a low, faint, and continuous sound

potential—something that can develop and become actual

scramble—to move with urgency or panic

spectators—people who look on at a sports event

strategy—a careful plan or method

DISCUSSION QUESTIONS

1. At the beginning of the story when playing a match against Trey, Deion confidently thinks, *I own him.* We don't hear him think that again until the very end of the story. How and why does Deion struggle to regain his confidence throughout the story?

2. Deion struggles with accepting his stepdad, Terry, as part of his family. How does that change by the end of the story? Have you ever struggled with changing family dynamics?

3. In Chapter 9, Deion's stepdad tells Deion that he and Cole play for different reasons. Deion plays to win while Cole plays for something to do. What does he mean? Do you think that playing one way is better than the other?